THE NIGHT ONES

by Patricia Grossman   illustrated by Lydia Dabcovich

SCHOLASTIC INC.

New York   Toronto   London   Auckland   Sydney

Text copyright © 1991 by Patricia Grossman.
Illustrations copyright © 1991 by Lydia Dabcovich.
All rights reserved. Published by Scholastic Inc., 555 Broadway,
New York, NY 10012, by arrangement with Harcourt Brace & Company.
The illustrations in this book were done in markers
and Prismacolor pencils on tissue paper.
The display type was set in Gill Sans Medium.
The text type was set in Gill Sans Medium.
Designed by Judythe Sieck.
Printed in the U.S.A.
ISBN 0-590-48754-X

1 2 3 4 5 6 7 8 9 10   14   01 00 99 98 97 96 95 94

For my niece, Rachel —P. G.   *For Mu* —L. D.

When the night bus arrives at the stop the night ones get off and turn down the street.

They walk until Clarence says good night

and goes off to clean important rooms.

Four move along until it is time for Honey to leave

and begin rolling her night away.

Three continue until Porter says farewell

and goes to greet travelers from near and far.

Two walk steadily along

until Amelia catches another bus,

which takes her to her office,

the sky.

Only Cap is left and he runs to the docks,

where a ship heads in, sailing west.

The night ones stay in their places . . .

19

. . .

. . .

. . .

. . . until morning.

Then Cap watches a ship head out, sailing east;

Amelia turns her back on the office that circles the world;

Porter tips his hat to Oscar, who will hold the door all day;

Honey greets the avenue with a heavenly smell;

and Clarence spins himself out the last important door.

When the night ones reach their stop

the night bus pulls away to make room for the morning bus,

which takes them home.